The Mystery of Mrs Raven

Written by Florence Whelon and the
Growing Learners Team

Illustrated by Richard Heathcote

ISBN-13: 978-1519667885
ISBN-10: 1519667884

DEDICATION AND ACKNOWLEDGEMENTS

For all the children, students, teachers and parents
we have worked with.

We would like to express our gratitude for the Higher
Education Innovation Funding from the University of
Portsmouth which has enabled us to write this book.

THE MYSTERY OF MRS RAVEN

Jo sat quietly on the edge of the rock hard chair in the corner of the classroom. A wind chime tinkled softly as it spun around in the September breeze. There were rows of numbers everywhere, written in a thick black print. Each wall seemed to be covered in multiplications and divisions and subtractions. When she looked outside, she saw that there was a small piece of glass embedded into the window. It was decorated with a woman's face, and depending on how you looked at it, she was either smiling or snarling. Her eyes were black and cold looking. No sunshine dared to touch it, and just looking at it made Jo shudder. It was horrible that she had ended up here. Out of all the places.

Dad had said that this school was supposed to be a fresh start.

"You can *learn* here," he had said as they were driving away from London, Jo's former home. Dad always emphasised words when they were meant to be important. This school wasn't important, though. It meant nothing to her. The countryside alone was quite peaceful, but it was also very boring. Nothing interesting ever seemed to happen. The outside world only really seemed to come alive when Jo was with her friends. You couldn't play with a flower or go on adventures only with the wind for company. It just wasn't right. Now, what was even worse was that she was forced to sit indoors whilst all the other kids went off and gossiped outside. But Jo was not allowed to do that. Oh no. She slowly closed her eyes and Mrs Raven's voice crept into her head like a little black spider.

Mrs Raven was her new teacher. She smelt dusty. She had long grey hair that snaked down her back like a piece of wool and her eyes were as grey as an owl's feather. She always wore a coat that was dark blue. It was the same colour as how Jo imagined the sea would look at night. It was such a long coat that no one could see her shoes. Jo wondered if maybe she just had socks on underneath, or maybe some cosy slippers. That was unlikely though, because Mrs Raven always complained that it was too cold in the classroom, even if the heating was turned right up and it felt like Jo's pen was going to melt.

However, the very worst thing about Mrs Raven was that she called Jo by her full name. No one, except when her parents were really, *really* angry, called Jo by her first name. It made her feel like she was in a permanent state of trouble. Actually, Jo *was* in trouble this morning, which was why she was now indoors staring at the creepy glass woman in the first place. It had all started with the test.

"*No,* Jocelyn," Mrs Raven had whispered, as if every word were poison, "You *cannot* go outside and *play* if you do not complete the test to the correct standard. You will stay *indoors.*"

Huh! Jo had never heard anything like it before. All the other kids had giggled and nudged each other. That's the new girl, they snickered, and she can't even pass one test! Still, at least they were all gone now, for fifteen minutes. The wind chime sang another little tune as a fiercer breeze swept across the playground outside. She missed her friends in London. At her old school, she had been the leader, the cool cat of the group.

Jo thought back to the summer. Everything had been coated in sunshine syrup, without a whisker of an Autumn breeze. There were no crosses, unlike on the test paper which lay on her desk. The summer had been one giant tick. Her school before might as well have had a big golden, glittery star floating above it, announcing to the world that it was the Best School Ever. Her old friends wouldn't have given a fig if she had got one or two questions wrong. OK, maybe five or six. Out of seven. They would have laughed, but in a kind way. Then they would have all gone out to look for bugs that lay hidden in the warm soil or who flew amongst the trees. Nature was a lot more fun with friends.

Sometimes, Jo wished that she was like a bug. Moths were her favourite. Jo had read a lot about them. There used to be a type of moth that was creamy coloured. They moved to the big city, where the air was thick with smoke and dust. Jo wondered if the moths could breathe properly, or if their tiny lungs were permanently cloudy. The moths got in a lot of trouble because they could be seen pretty easily, and a lot of them got eaten. It was like your whole family being eaten up, Jo thought. Their numbers began to dwindle, and fast. They needed a plan. And, eventually, they came up with one. Over time, the moths became darker. The colour of smoke and dust. Until they were no longer the colour of cream. They had become the chameleons of the bug world, and they lived happily ever after in the palace of darkness that is London. Or something like that. Jo sighed and closed her eyes again. Her eyelids were warm and dark. She missed London. During the day, she tried to not think about it, but thoughts were a lot like the game of Grandma's footsteps. As soon as you turned your back on them, they crept up on you. She dreamed of London. Unfortunately, when she woke and heard the cockerel's increasingly annoying squawking and the cows mooing, the country became her reality.

The school bell rang out. Her heart seemed to drop into her tummy. Oh no. Why couldn't they stay out there forever? The dim thud of a thousand footsteps seemed to run towards her.

The voice of Mrs Raven shattered her thoughts:

"*Why* do you have your eyes closed, Jocelyn? You are *not* going to find the answers there!" Jo silently groaned and opened her eyes. I don't care about the test, she thought. One test doesn't prove anything, except if you have nice handwriting or not. She shuffled uncomfortably on the chair. All the kids had sat down and were looking obediently at the board, where Mrs Raven was writing. They were like faceless soldiers wrapped up in their blue and black uniform. She noticed one boy at the back who was quietly trying to blend in with the carpet.

Mrs Raven turned to face the class. She wrapped her coat tighter round her. She was very, very tall with skin the colour of milk. She smiled. Her teeth were very white and sharp looking.

"I have four questions for everyone!" She announced, "I also have four bars of chocolate. Whoever answers the questions right will get one!" The classroom seemed to quiver. No one looked happy. Jo was confused. Why was no one jumping at the chance to learn more stuff? Why did a sudden cloak of gloom enshroud them?

"OK. First question. We'll start off nice and easy. *Everybody* should already know this. What is the largest ocean in the world?"

There was a silence. Jo thought hard but there was only one ocean that she could think of. When the quietness almost got too much to bear, she put her hand up. She was the only one in the whole of the class.

"Yes, Jocelyn?" Mrs Raven said with a tinge of reluctance in her voice. It was not a good sign, but Jo was determined.

"Is it the unwell sea?" She asked.

Mrs Raven narrowed her eyes.

"The. Unwell. Sea," She announced, sweeping her eyes over the classroom. The silence had been replaced by soft laughing. Mrs Raven flicked her cold, grey eyes back to Jo.

"I don't think so, dear," she said. "There is a book on oceans in the school library. I suggest you read it, although you should already know this most *basic* information."

At that moment, Jo would have given anything to magic herself into a moth and fly away. "Moving on..." said Mrs Raven darkly,

"I still have four chocolate bars! Let me choose someone who *is* going to know it.....Leo! Tell us, what is the largest ocean in the world?"

She menacingly waved the chocolate at the boy who had clearly failed to disguise himself as the carpet. He looked up, fear etched into his face. Jo almost felt sorry for him, but then she realised that he was probably like all the others. Jo found herself holding her breath.

"It's the Pacific," Leo whispered.

Mrs Raven grinned. Now she looked truly terrifying. Jo hoped that she would never grin like that at her. She suspected that it was more likely that an unwell sea really did exist than that happening. Leo didn't smile back. He looked relieved. Everyone else looked slightly disappointed. It was like they wanted him to get it wrong.

"That's correct, very clever Leo! Come and get your prize!"

Leo jumped up so quickly that he stumbled

a bit. When he went to collect his chocolate, a couple of the kids glared him. It made Jo feel sad. It looked like she wasn't the only one who wasn't popular. Mrs Raven then told them that there would be another test tomorrow. Whoever did the best would get the next chocolate bar. That made Jo feel even sadder. She could have been promised a thousand chocolate bars, but she still would rather not do another one of Mrs Raven's tests.

Finally school finished. Jo's mind ached, but she was determined to learn more about oceans. She wasn't going to let Mrs Raven put her off learning about anything.

The library was lovely and big, with rows and rows of books as tall as a giant giraffe. The librarian was nice, although she seemed lost in her own paper filled world. She pointed dreamily to a dark corner of the room.

There was no one about. The books were all blue and green, with fanged sea monsters and creepy octopuses. Eurgh. Jo didn't like octopuses at all. Instead, she picked out a huge black book, with gold writing that announced: OCEANS OF THE WORLD. Inside, it read: water is a fascinating element, able to slip through the tiniest cracks and yet it can also develop into an ocean, which covers 71% of the Earth's surface! Water is an exceptionally important life source. Without water, we wouldn't exist. With water, we can thrive. In fact, we are made up of up to 75% of water, which shows just how important it is.

Big deal, thought Jo. She did like the idea of how the smallest drop of water could squeeze through the rocks. The biggest ocean, she read, is the Pacific. Well, now I know for sure, thought Jo. She wondered if maybe she could be considered smart now. Or did people just get picked to be smart, when they were born? Did someone look down and say, yes that child is going to be smart, or no, that child is not going to be smart. And that was the end of that? Were you born knowing exactly which ocean was the largest, or the answer to all the Maths problems? Jo couldn't really answer these questions, but she knew that she would rather be an explorer of knowledge than someone who got it right all the time. Mrs Raven didn't seem to see it that way, though. Being smart just reminded her of the test and being laughed at. And even if you were considered clever, it didn't mean that others automatically liked you. Just then, she heard a noise, like a little mouse. She had been so deep in thought that she hadn't noticed a small figure creeping up to her. It was Leo.

"Hello," Jo said softly. Leo smiled the smallest smile possible back.

"Are you reading?" he whispered.

"Yeah," replied Jo, wondering why their voices were so quiet, "about oceans."

Leo cast his eyes downward. He nodded.

"Sometimes I read too. Although," he added hastily, "I already know most of it."

Jo was confused. Did Leo drink a knowledge potion or something? She looked back down at her book, but when she looked up he was gone. All that remained was a single chocolate bar on the table. Had Leo had forgotten it? Jo thought about rushing after him to give it back. Or, perhaps, it was an unofficial welcome into the school.

The next day, it took all the effort in the world for Jo to get out of bed. Her dad came in and threw the curtains open in the most dramatic way possible.

"Up, up, up!" he bellowed. Jo did not want to get up, and it had nothing to do with being a lazy bones. She could almost see Mrs Raven preparing for another day at school, writing on the whiteboard and perfecting questions for the new test. She wished that she could hide under the covers all day.

Outside, it was raining. Jo let the tiny drops fall into the palm of her hands. She stuck out her tongue. The water was refreshing. When she got inside the classroom, the woman who was painted into the glass looked as if she had tears running down her cheeks. Jo knew how she felt. The tests were already laid out on their desks. The words were all squiggly, as if they were Arabic or Chinese.

At least, that's how they looked at first. Then they merged into more familiar words, like they were the shape shifters of letters. Mrs Raven was watching her. She was such a dragon, thought Jo. But instead of Mrs Raven hissing flames, she breathed tests. Tests that were flames licked with questions about stuff that Jo had never even heard about. Jo smiled sweetly at Mrs Raven, and in response, Mrs Raven stretched her mouth into a tight, false grin like a clown. Her coat, as ever, was wrapped tightly around her. Today, her grey hair was up in a bun, and some loose bits of hair danced around her face like mouse tails made of wool.

"Good Morning, class!" she said, and the class obediently replied. Jo did not, because it was not a good morning. It was a horrible morning.

"Now, as you can see, we are going to start off this *beautiful* day with a quick test!" said Mrs Raven brightly. Jo looked down at the questions which lined her sheet of paper. Her test seemed to shimmer with failure. Jo felt suddenly very afraid. What if she failed? What if Mrs Raven called her up and told everyone, and they all laughed at her again? She couldn't bear the thought of that happening again. It was bad enough the first time. It wasn't benefitting anyone. Except those in the class who fed off misery pie, of which Mrs Raven seemed to serve up every slice. But then Jo had to remember; she was not a sorceress of learning who could magic up all the answers. She was here to learn. I have to keep thinking that, she thought to herself. She could feel Mrs Raven looking at her, those grey eyes seeming to peer right into Jo's brain. She suddenly shivered. It *was* unusually cold in here, although she couldn't figure out why.

Everyone started the test. The questions were completely random, but the thing that they all had in common was that they were really hard. Mrs Raven told the class that, during their break, she would mark all the tests and then write all the results down in her test book. It sounded like no fun, but at least Jo got to have a break this time. Being away from the others on the first day had been OK, but she had to try and get along with them at some point. She was determined to try and make new friends.

Finally, the test was over. Jo could almost hear her pen let out a little sigh when she stopped writing. She knew that she had done pretty badly. But it wouldn't be the end of the world. After all, she could always improve. Mrs Raven let them all out of the class. Luckily, it had stopped raining, and the sun seemed to shyly peer out from under the clouds. Some of the kids weren't so bad after all. One of the girls in her class came up to her just as break had started and murmured, in a dark voice:

"Would you like to hear a secret?" Jo thought about it for half a second.

"OK," she whispered back. The girl nodded slowly and her eyes seemed to glitter.

"There is," she began, leaning in closer to Jo, "a ghost in the P.E. shed."

"Oh," replied Jo, "really?"

"Yes!" she replied, "Would you like to go and see it?"

"Sure," said Jo. She wasn't quite sure what this girl was playing at, but she was happy to go along with it for now. The girl snuck along to the back of the playground, where there was a big oak tree and a fairly large shed. Jo didn't even know her name. But she still followed her, curious to see this ghost. The girl looked once over her shoulder and then pulled Jo into the shed and quickly closed the door.

"By the way," the girl said, "my name's Becky." Becky had long, brown hair and big, round eyes. She looked quite magical to Jo, although she couldn't put her finger on it as to why. She looked around. If there was a ghost, it didn't seem to want to come out. It smelt like mothballs and there was only a tiny window. She almost fell over a basketball.

"Here is where it is. I saw it last time, I really did!"

Jo raised her eyebrows. "Sure!" she replied. Becky's eyes widened.

"I really did! It was so spooky. Of course, I had heard the rumours but I didn't believe them until recently".

"What rumours?" asked Jo.

"Well, basically, it was an athlete before it became a ghost..."

"OK..."

"They were, like, the best athlete ever. EVER. I can't actually remember what they did, but they were really good. Like, amazing!" Becky's eyes shined in the darkness of the shed.

"And then, something happened to them," she continued, "something *mysterious*. They stopped winning everything. They were never really the same after that, so they kind of just faded away…" Becky dramatically pretended to faint by putting her hands over her eyes and slowing dropping down to the floor. When Jo didn't react, Becky took one hand away, so only one sparkling eye could be seen. Jo raised her eyebrows.

"It is usually here, I swear. We can come back another time, I guess. You'll learn, this is a school full of weird stuff." Becky jumped up and ran out of the shed, leaving Jo very bewildered. Did this mean that she had made a new friend?

The bell rang out shrilly. It was time to go back inside, to the test that was waiting for her. Jo was not looking forward to her test results. No one else looked too thrilled, either. She noticed that Leo sank into the room without looking up once. He had his head down and his hands in his pockets. He sat down, in his usual place at the back of the classroom. He didn't look too upset, but who knew how he was truly feeling? Jo thought that it would be much easier if people had a little tag, like a balloon, above their heads which showed their true feelings. I'm happy, one might say, with a big smile. I'm confused, for another. Or, maybe, one that said: I may seem happy but I'm actually pretty sad. That would be a very useful one. She wondered how many people in the room felt that way. She felt bad that she hadn't been with him during break. In fact, she had barely seen him at all. She wondered if maybe he had friends from other years. Or no friends. Or maybe friends who were friendly ghosts.

    Mrs Raven walked in. She most certainly didn't need a feelings balloon above her head. Instead, she looked as if all the rain from the morning had been poured on to her. Her mouth was like a wrinkled rosebud. When she spoke, her voice was strained, "Everyone, I have your test results. Now, what I am going to do is pair you all up depending on your score. For example, the highest scorer will go with the lowest and so forth. Understand?"

The class murmured in reply. Jo felt butterflies flap lazily in her stomach. This was not good. Mrs Raven produced a list with a neat, small script on it. For a brief moment, Jo wondered if Mrs Raven ever spoke to the other teachers at break, or if she simply sat in a small room somewhere, shivering in her coat and writing the crosses or ticks which seemed so important to her. But the thought was soon gone, replaced by the sound of blood running in her veins.

"The first pair," said Mrs Raven, "are Jocelyn and Leo."

Oh well, thought Jo, trying to ignore her heart sinking. She was disappointed but it wasn't as if she was going to paint herself blue because of it. It was weird how one test result could affect you. Leo was so lucky, being naturally smart.

"Jocelyn, can you go and chat with Leo please. You can help him try and improve for next time."

Did Jo hear her right?

"But, Mrs Raven, why am I helping Leo? I thought that I failed the test?"

Mrs Raven shook her head, and her tendrils of hair bounced against her chalky skin.

"You did the best, Jocelyn," said Mrs Raven, "unfortunately, Leo didn't do so well. Now, pair up."

When neither of them moved, Mrs Raven clapped her hands together. It made a sound that seemed to flow out towards the class and then slowly fade as it reached Jo's ears. It sounded a bit like her heart thumping, slowly but steadily. Was this all a big joke? Maybe all that reading she had done yesterday had made a difference. Suddenly, she felt a burst of happiness, like a firework. But then she looked over at Leo. He had made himself even smaller. A tear, like a drop of the Pacific, rolled quietly down one cheek, before he hurriedly wiped it away. Jo moved closer to him, and he seemed to shrink away.

"Shall we look at our answers?" said Jo, cautiously. There was no response. Leo didn't blink. He was like a faded picture. Why was he so affected by one test? She could see some of his answers from where she was sitting. To her surprise, his answers weren't even close to being right, anyone could see that. For some, he hadn't put down anything. Jo looked at Leo quizzically. Leo peeped back at her, his eyes sorrowful.

"I knew I couldn't do it," he said, his voice laden with despair, "I knew I wasn't smart."

The sound of other pupils talking about their tests played about them like musical words, but it felt like Jo was trapped in a bubble with Leo. She tried to say that it wasn't true, that no one got it perfect all the time. But then a girl came over, and it was like she stabbed her finger right through the bubble.

"Not so great this time, Leo?" she said, her eyes narrowing until they resembled slits of emerald green.

"I always knew you weren't truly smart," she added, "and as for you," she snarled, turning to Jo, "you just got lucky this time. You should probably make the most of this moment because when the next test comes up, you'll be just the same as *him*." With one final evil look, the girl walked off to the other side of the classroom. Jo sighed.

"Take no notice of her," she whispered softly to Leo, who looked even more crushed.

"She is right though," he replied, "just look at my test. I've failed the whole thing!"

Jo shook her head. "That's not true. Yesterday I didn't know a couple of answers, but so what? You can't do great all of the time. You can always improve though, *especially* when you feel like giving up."

"I am going to give up," said Leo.

"You can't!" said Jo, but Leo wasn't listening. Instead, he muttered something that Jo couldn't quite hear. She folded her test until the answers were hidden and tried to be as helpful as she could. She didn't quite believe what she was going to say, but it was something that her dad used to tell her, and most dads seemed to know what they were talking about.

"I know you probably won't listen," said Jo, "but I'll say it anyway." Leo twitched, which Jo took as a sign that he was listening. "I guess..." Jo started, "learning is kind of like a magic trick. When it comes to the final performance, everyone thinks that it really *is* magic. It looks like you haven't done anything, and that it all comes naturally..."

"But I thought that the whole point of magic is that it does come naturally. You wouldn't be a very good magician if things went wrong all the time?" Interrupted Leo.

"That's where you are wrong" said Jo "The whole point of magic is that is *seems* like magic. Do you know any card tricks"?

"Yeah, I love doing card tricks" said Leo.

"How did you learn how to do them?" asked Jo.

"My dad taught me some" answered Leo.

"Well, that's exactly my point" said Jo, "You don't just start off knowing how to pull off a card trick. It looks like magic when someone shows you, and then you have to learn how it is done if you want to do it yourself. You work at it. You wouldn't give up halfway and then say, well, a *true* magician would just know how to do it naturally, because that's not the case. And, besides, you want the trick to be as smooth as possible, and that will always take a little effort and practice. Right?"

"I guess" replied Leo. "I still feel rubbish though" he said softly. He looked at his test, at the crosses which accompanied every question.

"I know," said Jo, thinking back to her first day. "But when things go wrong or seem hard, that doesn't mean you won't succeed eventually. You just need to put your all into it. The only way you really fail at something is when you give up trying."

With that, the bell for home time rang, and Leo jumped up and was out of the classroom in two blinks. When Jo got up too, she saw that Mrs Raven was standing by the door. She was looking at Jo. And she was smiling. Her midnight blue coat seemed to sparkle. There was something strange about her, though. It wasn't until Jo had walked out of the door that she realised. Mrs Raven's grey eyes were now completely black.

The next day, it was almost time for Jo's third day at school. She had a weird feeling about today. As she reached the school gates, dad gave her a hug.

"Make the most of today," he whispered, "hopefully it will be better!" Jo nodded in reply.

"See you at three," dad added, "be good!" Then he walked one way and Jo went the other, until she was, once again, deep into the belly of the school.

When she got into the classroom, the atmosphere felt different. Everyone was looking at the whiteboard with a confused look in their eyes. When Jo looked, she saw why. There was a very strange sentence on the whiteboard. It said: Why are foxes and pumpkins both orange? Jo's first thought was that it was a very odd question. There were no Maths questions or Geography puzzles. The room felt warmer, a little toastier. Where was Mrs Raven?

Leo came in. To Jo's surprise, he came and sat down next to her. He smiled. "Hi, Jo," he said. Jo grinned back.

"Hi, Leo!" she replied, relieved that he seemed to be much happier than the day before.

"I like this question," Leo said, "it doesn't feel like something that Mrs Raven would write. Maybe she's given up the tests for today," he added hopefully.

"One test free day would be good," said Jo, "although I'm not sure why foxes and pumpkins are the same colour. Maybe it is because there are only so many colours to go around?"

Leo nodded in agreement. "Maybe it's because orange is a nice, happy colour?" he queried.

"Yeah!" replied Jo, "like the sun always makes me happy, and those ice creams that are orange flavoured are the best."

Just then, she felt the room darken as the mean girl came and sat down next to her. Jo smiled, trying to fulfil her promise of today being a good day, but the girl didn't react.

"I wouldn't bother answering this question," she said, nastily, "only clever people would get it. You can try all you want, but you'll either be smart enough to know it or you won't." Jo just shrugged. The idea that she was either smart or wasn't didn't make any sense to her by now. The mind seemed like a vine that never stopped growing.

"That's not true," said Leo, suddenly. Jo looked at him. Even he looked surprised that he had spoken up. The girl sneered.

"Oh, really? You would say that, wouldn't you."

"It's true!" added Jo.

"Progress, not perfection" said Leo triumphantly. Jo was impressed. The girl rolled her eyes.

"Whatever," she muttered, before walking off. Jo watched her retreating back with glittering eyes. Leo laughed, for the first time since Jo had met him.

"I'm sure she's nice really," he said. Jo waved as Becky came in. Just behind her was another teacher. There was still no sign of Mrs Raven, which was very odd.

This new teacher seemed brighter and more colourful, as if someone had dipped her soul in a rainbow of colours. She walked like a ballerina who was performing in a competition. Even her voice was softer. Jo felt very suspicious.

"Good morning, class!" the teacher began. Her eyes fell on Jo. "Hello! Its Jocelyn isn't it? Or would you preferred to be called Jo?"

Jo nodded, very slowly, trying to understand what was happening. The teacher beamed. Her smile could have won a prize for happiness.

"Welcome, Jo! I'm Mrs Nutbean, your new teacher. I'm sorry that I wasn't here on your first day. I do hope that the supply teacher was welcoming. I'm sure she was."

"She was an interesting person," Jo replied quietly. Things were starting to make sense now. Or were they? Why had Mrs Raven vanished without saying goodbye?

"So, foxes, pumpkins. They are both orange. Why do you think that is?" Mrs Nutbean asked.

The girl next to Jo was silent. Jo could almost feel the girl willing her to get the answer wrong. But Jo didn't care. She didn't want to be wrong. But then, on the other hand, maybe she could give a correct answer. And even if she wasn't right, she could still say that she had tried. Anything would be better than staying silent and locked in a world where to fail once would be to fail altogether.

"Is it because they are bright, and orange is easy to spot?" Jo answered. Mrs Nutbean nodded thoughtfully.

"That's a very thoughtful answer!" she said. "What do you think, Leo?"

There was a pause. Jo willed Leo silently on. Eventually, he spoke out. "It could be because the orange is a warning to predators? Although I'm not sure if a pumpkin has any predators..." Everyone, including Leo, laughed.

"That's a great answer!" replied Mrs Nutbean with a big smile on her face. "The thing about this question," she continued "is that there isn't really a *right* answer, but there are lots of great answers. I just wanted you to all experience being asked a question that you wouldn't know the answer to, as this is what learning is all about; searching for answers that we don't yet know. Nobody knows the answer to every question, but the person who knows the most is the person who searches for the most. You should always search for as many answers as possible, even if they don't seem particularly successful. Never settle for one answer when there are many possibilities."

Jo couldn't have agreed more. But she had one more question that she wanted to ask. "Mrs Nutbean? Where did Mrs Raven go?" she asked.

Mrs Nutbean frowned. "Mrs Raven? Don't you mean Mrs Swan?" Jo shook her head.

The class went quiet. Mrs Nutbean frowned, but her eyes still sparkled. "We don't have a Mrs Raven here," she said. "Our supply teacher is Mrs Swan, she is the one who would have been teaching you. Of course," she added, "we do have a Mrs Raven over here!" Mrs Nutbean walked over to the painting of the woman in the glass.

"We call this lady Mrs Raven. No one knows how she ended up being called that, perhaps she named herself! I'll have to talk to Mrs Swan and see why she decided to call herself Mrs Raven.

A very odd trick, I suppose!" Leo and Jo looked at each other.

"I knew that there was something strange about Mrs Raven!" whispered Leo.

"It's a mystery!" replied Jo.

Then, before anyone could ask any more about Mrs Raven, Mrs Nutbean asked everyone to get into pairs and discuss the differences between foxes and pumpkins. It was fun, and the morning seemed to go very quickly.

Outside, the weak sun shone a slither of light on the windows. The woman painted on the glass seemed to be glowing.

QUESTIONS FOR DISCUSSION

Why did Jo think that her new school 'wasn't important' and state that it 'meant nothing to her'?

The descriptions of Mrs Raven include words like 'spider', 'dusty', 'snaked' and 'cold'. Why do you think this might be? How would you feel if Mrs Raven was your teacher?

How do you think Jo felt when she was told that she couldn't go outside at play time because she hadn't done well enough on her test?

Why do you think Jo wished she was like a bug? And what was it about the moth that she liked so much? Why?

Jo noticed that Leo was trying to 'blend in with the carpet'. Why do you think this might be?

Jo was confused that no one in the class was jumping at the chance to learn. Why do you think this was? Why did everyone seem so scared when Mrs Raven asked a question? How do you think the prize chocolate bars made them feel?

How do you think Jo felt when she got her ocean question wrong?

When Jo was wondering about what it took for someone to be considered 'smart' – what did you think? Did you agree that people get picked to be smart when they are born?

Would you rather be an 'explorer of knowledge' or someone who just gets the answer right every time?

Leo admits to Jo that sometimes he reads too, but why does he quickly add that he 'already knows most of it?'

When Jo sat down to sit the next test, why did the words look all squiggly?

How do you think Jo felt when Becky came to talk to her at break time?

Did the ghost that Becky described have a Growth Mindset or a Fixed Mindset?

When Mrs Raven told Jo and Leo how they had done on the test, how do you think they both felt?

Why does Jo describe learning as being like a magic trick?

Jo tells Leo that 'the only way you really fail at something is when you give up trying.' Do you think she's right?

What was so interesting about the question Mrs Nutbean asked: 'Why are foxes and pumpkins both orange?'

Who do you think Mrs Raven was?

MINDSET LEARNING POINTS

At the beginning of the story, Jo presents a very negative view of her new school. Her dad is very positive about it, but Jo isn't convinced.

Jo seems particularly concerned about her new teacher, Mrs Raven, as well as the atmosphere in the classroom. The rest of the class seem scared of learning, which Jo doesn't understand. When Mrs Raven asks a question, Jo was the only pupil in the whole class who was willing to have a go at answering it. When she gets the answer wrong, Mrs Raven makes her feel embarrassed and stupid.

One reason for this might be because of the language that Mrs Raven uses with the class; she praises (and criticises) them based on their ability, for example: "That's correct, very clever Leo!" As a result, the class seem reluctant to engage in learning, they seem terrified of making a mistake and not looking clever. In contrast, Jo seems to be determined to try to improve and tackle challenges, as demonstrated when she goes to the library after school, stating that she would rather be an explorer of knowledge.

This hard work pays off; the next time they sit a test, Jo gets the highest mark in the class. For a while, she is very happy about doing the best. However, when Leo finds out that he didn't do very well, he is very disheartened and this makes Jo realise that doing the 'best' doesn't necessarily make you happy. Leo questions his ability 'I knew I wasn't smart' and wants to give up. Jo tries to reassure him by comparing learning to magic tricks; you have to practice and put lots of effort into it to get it right.

The atmosphere in the classroom really changes when Mrs Nutbean arrives. She is a warm and encouraging teacher. She asks questions that don't necessarily have a right answer but encourages her class to think and have a go. Leo suggests an answer and Mrs Nutbean responds positively. He seems convinced that learning can be fun!

ABOUT THE AUTHORS

Growing Learners are a team of educational research psychologists based at the University of Portsmouth. We are passionate about supporting schools and parents to improve their children's expectations and attainment, using evidence-based practice to support them to become resilient, confident and effective learners. Everything we offer is underpinned by psychology and education theory, and applied research showing what works.

In designing materials for our intervention packages, we quickly realised that there was a need for children's story books which emphasise the Growth Mindset approach. We therefore called upon Florence Whelon, who at the time was a Creative Writing student at the university, to come and work with us. We have since written a number of wonderful children's stories together embracing this approach.

Find out more at: http://www.port.ac.uk/department-of-psychology/community-collaboration/growing-learners/

Printed in Great Britain
by Amazon